NEST

A short story that began
as an exhibition

Workshop Press: Leeds

Nest

© 2020 by the author of this book Garry Barker.

This edition published 2020 by Workshop Press: Leeds
10 Newton Grove, Leeds, LS7 4HW

NEST

This is a story about wisdom and folly, about a quest and a voyage across the seas, about the birthing of monstrous things, of wastefulness and carbon chains and of how kindness can grow and of how people can be thoughtless, of dreams and nightmares and of how imagination creates new life.

This is a tale of a creature made of bits of tat and odds and ends and all that stuff you find in bins. This is a story about a creation that no one wanted to think about, a thing with a mind of litter and a junk made body. It is a story about a creature no one noticed, but when you hear the salvage story of its birth, you will hopefully want to know more, so gather round quietly and listen, and I will tell a tale that will make you think about all those things that get thrown away and usually forgotten.

Last spring in a place beside a river, next to where the river was broken in two and sent across a weir, something wonderful happened. As the river divides, one half is forced to flow very slowly, and as it does so, its currents swirl around and around, and form small islands out of all the things a river carries along with it. The divided river then passes under a bridge heavy with many cars, and as it does so, one half of the river builds its banks with these water carried castoffs. It creates a quiet, under the bridge place, of rustling weeds and reeds and many other things, of nylon rope and rayon string and plastic things; of paper, card and broken toys and all those rubber balls we lose as children.

To that place, far beneath the noise of traffic, hidden from the dust and daily din, there came two swans that had always loved the river, as did their foremothers and their forefathers. It was spring, and there was something in the air, a feeling that a time had come for new things to be made. It was a time for swans to mate and build a nest. The cob, the male, was first to start, he pulled and tugged some broken twigs out of the reeds and laid them on the riverbank very close to the water's edge. Next he closed his beak around a plastic six-pack yoke and seeing that it was good for weaving, placed this over the broken twigs. Natural or man-made material, wood or plastic, for the swan it was all just stuff that could or couldn't be woven together. All he was concerned with was did it fit, could it be shaped into an idea of a nest? A pale blue plastic straw left over from a child's party, could be knitted into a curved nest wall made of an onion net, a broken computer circuit board, some string, twigs and water weed. What was an idea, was very quickly becoming a thing.

Now the mother swan, the pen, took over the process and lowered herself down over the middle of what was to become a nest and began to weave more tangled things around herself. She worked as swans have always done; she used her long neck to reach out all around herself and to pick up anything she could reach. She would pull and push whatever she picked up into the slowly growing idea of a nest; bits of broken reed, sticks and drying water weed; plastic bags, children's split rubber balls, polystyrene cups, scraps of textiles, a toothbrush, a broken spoon, and bits of tat and odds and ends and all the other stuff that humans throw away. This nest was a loving creation, if it was made from rubbish, this didn't matter, the swan had a new purpose for these things and she built with love. The nest grew bigger and stronger and as it became what it needed to be, anyone could see it was a singular and powerful form; it was not just a good nest, it was a new and rare thing that looked like a nest but which was far more than a nest. Eventually the pen settled, adjusted herself so that she fitted her body down into the nest and in her own time, when she was quite ready, laid one perfect egg; an egg that would over the next few days be joined by three others.

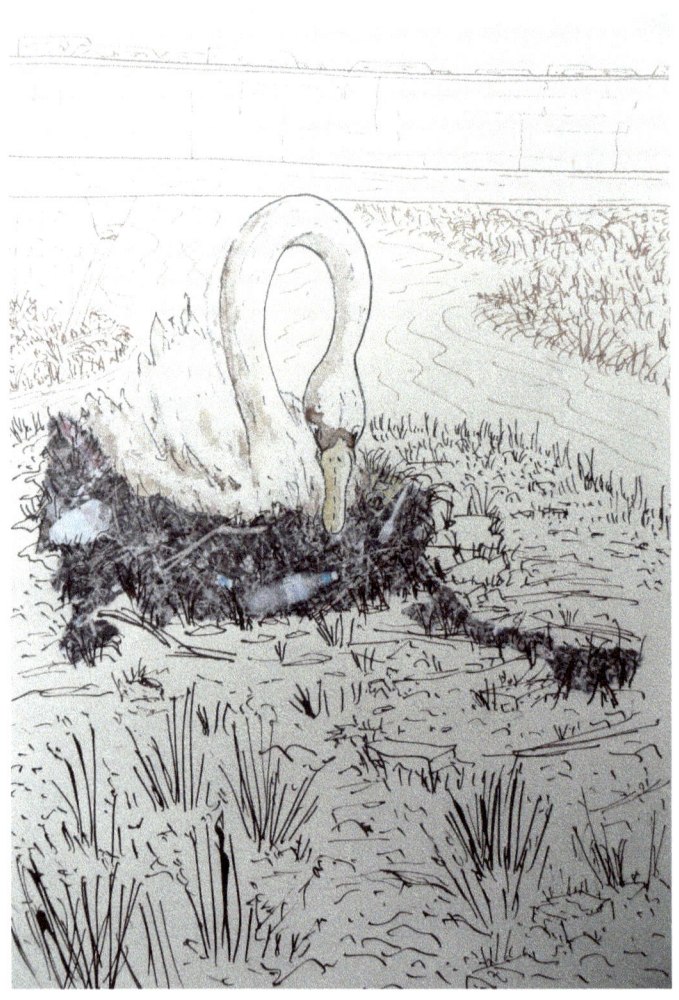

The two swans then took it in turns to sit on this nest, to keep the eggs warm and protected and as they did so, they continued to adjust the nest and rebuild it and care for it, weaving into it their love and care. For six long weeks, they shared their roles of protectors and shapers and carers, until the time that the eggs were ready to hatch.

The swans devoted their energies into making new life. But this year perhaps because they had to try even harder than usual, a miraculous something else was incubating, the nest itself was also woven into life. As the swans' attention was taken up with their brand new hatchlings, they never noticed another life awakening, but with a little help from the sun and the wind and the rains their love generated spark of life was being fanned into a flame. Every day when the sun came out and bathed the nest in light, its rays tweaked and changed a few things, stimulated atoms here and excited a few molecules there. Rain would often come and settle in the cracks and hollows of the nest, and as it was a slightly acid rain, it was a water that dissolved, re-shaped and twisted into being new connections and made links between chemicals and compounds. The wind would then swirl around the nest pushing oxygen into places it hadn't been before; blowing air into lungs that weren't lungs, until slowly and surely the nest began to breathe.

Summer passed and autumn came, the swans and their hatchlings moved on. The nest was filling with golden fallen leaves, and late autumn storms began to strip the remaining foliage from the trees. With the storms came pouring rain, and then the lightning. The wind blew hard, the rain came ever faster and the river rose. The lightning struck down into the ground, hissing as it struck water. It struck again, and again, each time getting closer and closer to the nest until just as the river pushed itself over the edges of its banks, KAPOW! The nest was struck by a great bolt of lightning, and at the same time it was swept away by rising river waters. It glowed and sizzled and smoked and looked as if it was about to burn, but just as a bright blue flame ran right around the circle of its form, a great wave of water pushed it down into the river and it was churned and turned and twisted upside down and right-side up, until it popped up from the river's depths with a WHOOSH! and with a great PLOP! it landed back on the river's edge and wobbled to its feet.

As it popped up into the air, some thoughts began to stir. The nest began to feel itself moving, for one moment it was swimming on the river's back like a new hatchling and the next it was in the air and now it was standing.

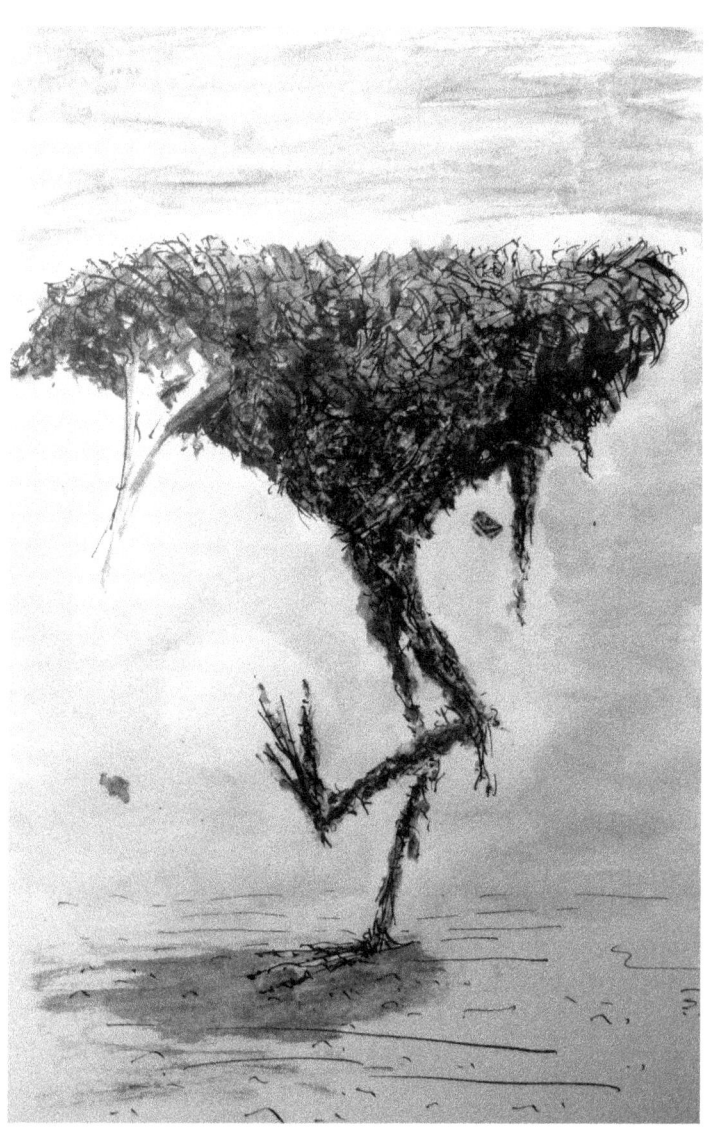

What was it, what was this thing, what was the doing that the thingness was part of? As first consciousness dawned the nest had only had a faint idea of itself. Am I a swanish thing, the nest thought? Am I a thing or a doing? Memories of broken and lost things and purposes ran through its wires and bits of string, thoughts of growing roots and sunlight emerged from tangled reeds and twisted twigs, it was a woven web of strange connections and connectors. Its net like mind connected to a polythene soul and a patched up body. Plastic lungs and muscles made of nylon string, were jerked into life by pulses made of electro-plastic quantum interactions, that tied a nerve like carbon web of body and mind together, while sticks and parts of broken toys attached themselves like legs or little wading paddles. As it looked out through an old doll's eyes with eyelash lids that sometimes even worked, it felt the sticks and broken biros that made up its bones and sensed the tins that now formed its belly and it gradually became aware of itself as something complete but incomplete; a thing that was yet to be an object.

The nest steadied itself and took a few steps. It walked on sticks and cardboard bits and plastic shards, all tangled up in netting. Its knees were socks all knitted in with copper wire and thread, but as it walked and looked about it saw that all around was sinking into water, the river was still rising and the nest's band new legs were far too weak to run away and hide.

As the waters rose the nest tried to stand taller, but it was soon standing in shallow water and then deeper water and then it could stand no more and it was swept away into the river again. But this time instead of sinking down into the water the old swan's nest and all its jumble of discarded bits now rode on the river. It was being swept along with all the other things that rivers carry with them and as it floated away its dreams began. This nest was a special nest. It was not just a jumbled up collection of plastic bags, with bits of stick and thrown away things that somehow could all float. This nest had a mind, a consciousness that was a product of love and care and the swans' rubbing and twisting together of bits of wire and string and fibre. It had an awareness, a concept of life made out of the turning back and forth and in and out of swans' beaks as they built and rebuilt the nest. It was a life that began as the sun and rain and wind replaced and moved and moved again the atoms and electrons and molecules of its swan woven body.

This was the life-form that was now drifting down the river, a creature that was a thing without a name, a thing of weavings and knots and an inside and an outside entangled with its inside structures.

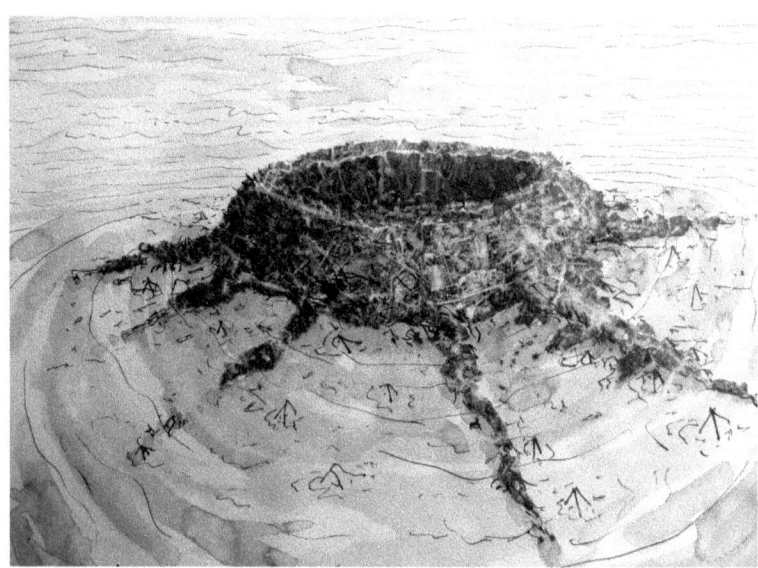

II

As it floated down the river the nest met others it could talk to. Some fish began to swim around its little plastic feelers, nosy things that soon began to talk of river tales and fishy family histories. They told the nest that a long time ago the river had been home to the songs of salmon and other fish but pollution from the factories along the river banks had led to the disappearance of the salmon and for a hundred years it had been for all the fish people a dead river, a place filled with sewage and chemicals, until it was so polluted that on each day of the week the water ran different colours and the river bottom looked just as if a grey woolen blanket had been spread all over everything, even over all the shiny man made things that got thrown into it; old bicycles, supermarket trollies, car wheels; everything had taken on the appearance of the same grey soft felt. This sight so worried the humans that lived alongside the river, that they began to clean the river up. Some humans even tried to stop factories tipping anything and everything into the river, they realised it wasn't good enough just to hope that the river would simply wash everything all away.

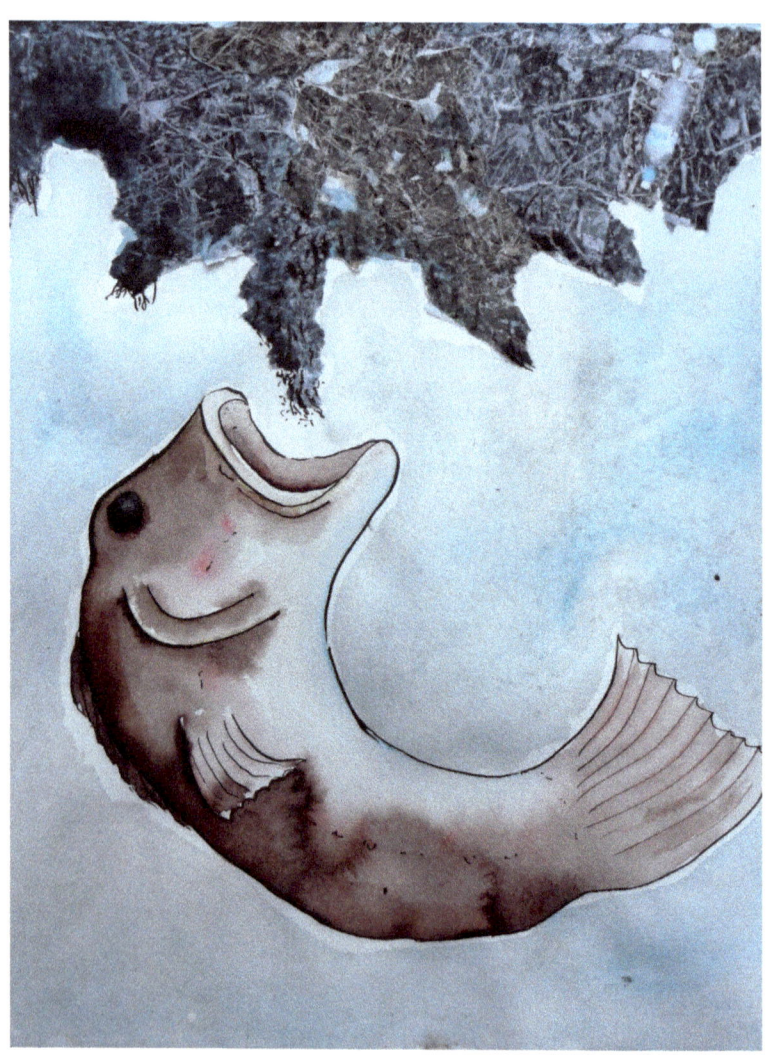

Gradually roach, then dace, then chub, then carp had returned to the river and even the occasional trout could now be found, but as yet no salmon had returned. Some fish were though worried about the nest, it looked too like all those other bits of broken plastic, nylon threads and glass shards that were always passing through their territory. But a nest is a nest after all and not all the fish were suspicious of it. One big fish, a fish from older times, a fish from out of the waters of the past, now appeared as if by magic and it somehow already knew what the nest really was. It looked right through to the heart of the nest and it swam up close and spoke in a burbling fishy tongue. "I see you are far away from where you should be little nest. You were born of the care for others, out of love and protection for their young. But something then went wrong, and you are not as you should be. There are no others here like you, some may look like you but they are not as you are. They pass through my world, and they travel far and wide, just as you will, but they are not as you are. I wish you well as a sentient being, but your story is only just beginning and it doesn't have an ending I can see. So travel on and as you do be kind and think of others, look for your friends and watch for those who would break you up and use you for their own ends".

Although the nest could think, it did not think as people think. Its mind was spread out amongst the various bits and pieces that were strung together to make it. But somehow it knew things, things like the melting point of various metals, of what electrical circuits were, of how plastics were created by making long carbon-based polymer chains from oil that came out from under the ground. But it had also learnt how swans made nests and how they cared for eggs; how rivers flow and what fresh water is like for things that live in the rivers; how fish swim and how rubbish floats or sinks. It was slowly finding its own voice, which was the sound of junk floating on water; of the noises made when things rub up against each other, of plastic against glass, of textiles moving over crumpled paper, a soft quiet crinkling, crunching, scratching and grating as surfaces touch and exchange atoms, all threaded together with the sounds that water makes as it moves around and through a woven net of debris. It thought slowly and carefully about what the ancient fish had told it, wishing it knew more about animal and vegetable lives and how they related to a mineral one. But it soon had other things to think about, life on the river was rarely dull and there were hidden dangers for all the river's creatures.

As the nest drifted through a dense clump of waterweed it heard a plaintive fishy voice crying, "Help me!" The nest followed the sound of this sad little voice, it twisted backwards and forwards through the weed until it found a beautiful carp that had caught its lip on the spike of an old fishhook. A fisherman's line had at some point been snapped and this thin transparent plastic line had wound its way around an old broken bicycle wheel, a wheel that in its rocking motion, was moving a hook attached to the line seductively backwards and forwards as the river currents flowed around it. The carp had mistaken the hook's movement for a meal and had only discovered its mistake at the last minute, but too late to avoid impaling its lip. Luckily the nest understood both metal and plastic, "I'll take that" said the nest, as it unpicked the hook from the line, and then eased the hook out through the hole it had made in the fish's lip. Once it had released the fish, it pushed the now released hook down into its own nest-work of plastic thread and old fishing lines, where the hook connected with nets and other lost materials and linked with them into the ever expanding nest mind. The fish was of course eternally grateful, and offered to help the nest out at any time of future need. As proof of its vow, the fish then coughed up from its stomach a beautiful shiny round smooth pebble and gave it to the nest. "If you are ever in trouble," it burbled, "just toss this stone into the water and wherever you are, I will send help".

The nest then waved goodbye to the carp and fast flowing currents swept it far away down the river. A river that was now getting wider and stronger, and which would soon join with another river, until eventually it flowed through a city of tall cathedral spires and even taller office blocks.

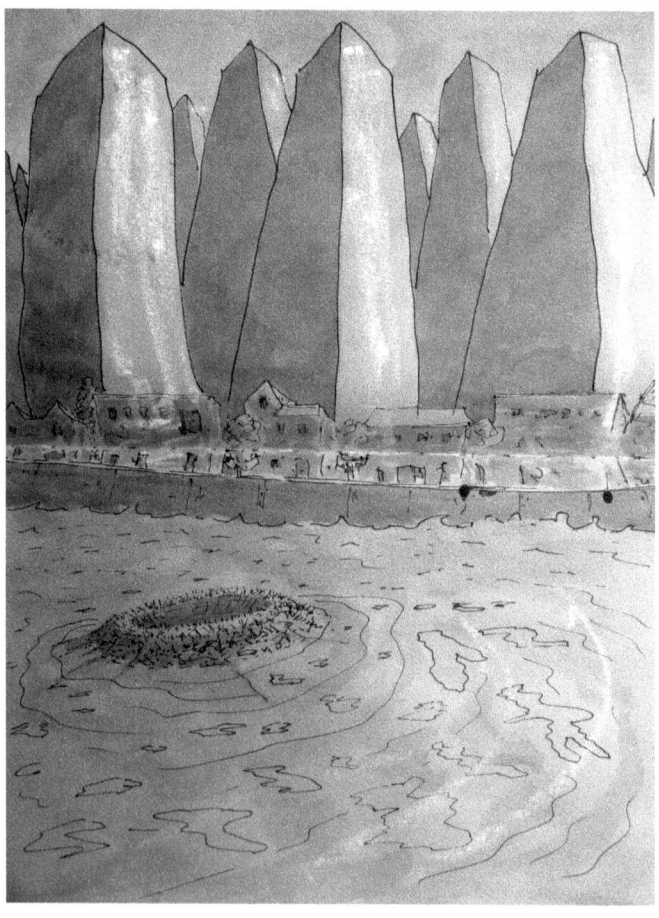

III

As the river flowed through the centre of the city the nest could taste the chemicals in the water changing; leads and salts, phosphates and nitrates and the complex subtle tastes of polychlorinated biphenyls. It drank them in and as it did it tasted their stories: it learnt about fields drenched with pesticides and of spillage from sewage works, it tasted tales of dilution and dissolution, of ignorance and arrogance. The nest drank them all in, sucked out the so-called pollution and as it did so, made itself much larger. It began to float past boats and under bridges, it looked on as people on a bridge stared down into the waters of the river, watching the nest as it watched them. The nest was yet another dense clump of rubbish drifting beneath them, something to aim at, as they dropped their empty crisp packets, threw their used water bottles and flicked their cigarette butts, into its now extended form.

The city was a weird place, more and more plastic bags, polystyrene fragments, bits of broken things and even brand new transparent polythene food containers came sweeping past. As they did so the nest opened its arms by floating out its nets and brought them into its body.

These discarded things had former lives and as they merged themselves into the body of the nest each one told a story of neglect and banishment, of obsolescence and of waste; stories that spurred the nest on to help its fellow things. If the nest could help it would and as it floated through the city it gradually became bigger and bigger as it touched and held and grasped one floating and lost piece of plastic after another. Soon the grand buildings that lined the riverside were however disappearing and trees and open land began to dominate the banks.

As it left the city behind, the nest spent time tying and knotting all the new bits of floating plastic into itself. Empty bleach bottles, water bottles, pop bottles and various cleaner containers; each one gave the nest a new problem to solve. Should it be fully netted in or simply tied around a handle? Is it better to push a stick through an open neck, or weave one round its middle? Just as it began to think about how to fasten several bottles together all at once, the nest became aware of a desperate cry. Splashing around by the river's edge was a baby otter, it was slowly drowning as it was being pulled under by a plastic six pack yoke, one hole of which had found its way around the otter's neck and another around a tree root that had worked its way out from the bank and down into the water.

Nest realised that it would have to act quickly. It forced its way through the thick weeds that lined the river bank, and as it did so it rearranged a few outlying feelers, brought some sharp edges into play and pulled a set of muscles into being that could make those edges snip and chop. It was quickly at the otter's side; "I'll take that," cried the nest, as it cut the plastic free of both the otter and the root. "Just the thing to tie myself together." Once the little baby otter was released it scrambled up and onto the nest, and as it did so it told the nest that it would be eternally grateful, and offered to help the nest out at any time of future need.

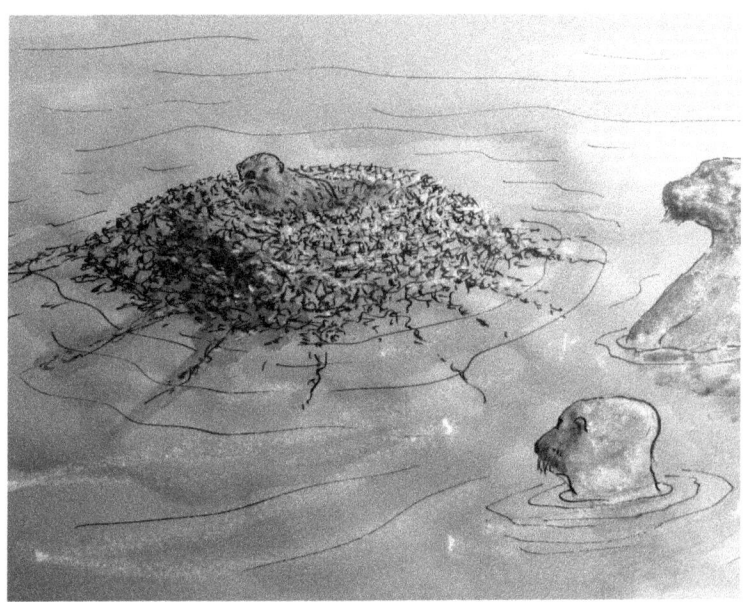

As proof of the otter's vow, it then coughed up from its stomach a beautifully polished round stone and gave it to the nest. "If you are ever in trouble", it said, "just toss this pebble into the water and help will come."

As the nest thanked the otter, the river currents took hold of it again and the tiny otter swam away to find its family. The nest now floated on, and as it did so, gradually the river slowed and widened. It was now very broad and it was hard to see the banks on either side. Something about the water had changed too; the creatures as they passed were not the same old river fish. The minerals in the water were changing and the nest felt the difference in its mineral mind, the water was now salty and the salt would form into crystals across and through its tangled and twisted together body. The nest could talk in many material languages and as salt collected in its nooks and crannies it spoke the tongue of seas and oceans, and of a place where creatures that were like the nest were found. But that was far away, so far away that the nest believed it was another world, one like the moon, or the stars above, a far off place that the nest began to imagine as a future home, a place of respite from the churning seas. The nest remembered what the old fish had told it about belonging somewhere far, far away. Could this place be where that somewhere was? Without really noticing when or how it got there, the nest found itself now floating in a sea. The way the water moved had changed, no longer were there fast and shallow currents moving things along, the swell of waves now tossed the nest upwards and then back down again. This made it harder for the nest to keep itself together but it had learnt a lot by then, so it took its strings and its nets and fishing lines and it wove them round and in and out and tied itself up tighter.

Occasionally more plastic objects and also wood and waterweed would touch upon its sides and when they did so it would welcome them into its body and fasten them into an ever growing mass. A mass that was moving and shaping itself with more purpose now, a mass that was looking for something.

Gradually the nest realised it was traveling anti clockwise in a huge body of salt water that surged and dropped and rose, and as it did, each swell and dip pushed it towards the south. The creatures passing by were also changing, jellyfish and dogfish, common seals, a rabbit fish and sharks. Skate and ray and lamprey, herring and pilchard and sprat, cod and mullet and sea bass all touched its various feelers and tasted its plastics and its metals, their various lips and mouth extensions longing for news of new foods or at least a change in diet. As they touched the nest they also passed on other thoughts of plastics now in stomachs and creatures suffocated in lost nets, stories of plastic encounters that the nest would go on the weave into its own tales of a rubbish life, its own story of forgotten trash.

IV

For several months the nest was carried along by the swell, it was slowly moving down the English coast, sometimes close to land and at other times far out at sea. At one point as it neared the shore it heard a desperate cry, it looked down below and there it spied an octopus trapped in wire netting that was itself entangled in seaweed. The octopus was a fully-grown and powerful creature, but even with all its eight arms and wonderful flexibility it couldn't un-entangle itself from the netting. But the nest could now shape itself into whatever it wanted to and it extended itself into arm like pincers, a shape that could snip through metal wire and at the same time hold it and bend it. "I'll take that," cried the nest, and it carefully untangled the netting from both the seaweed and the octopus, and as it did so it pulled the netting into itself, thinking "I could always do with a bit more iron, I was feeling a bit anaemic".

On being released, the very grateful octopus offered to help the nest out in any time of future need and as proof of the vow, it then coughed up from its stomach a beautiful round pebble and gave it to the nest. "If you are ever in trouble", it said, "just toss this stone into the water and help will come."

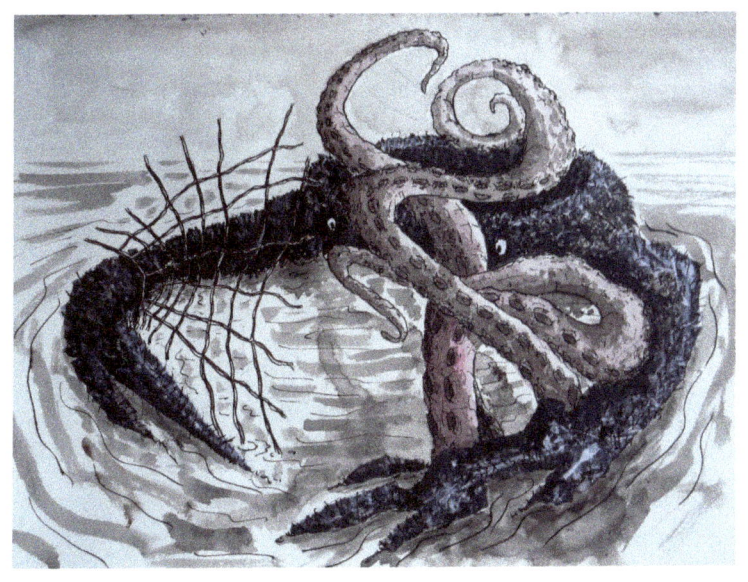

The sea soon swept the nest away and for several days it headed east and then as the winds changed direction and the currents followed suit it began to drift north, making its way in a huge circular movement that took it out into the dark seas that swept past Norway. The water had now become very cold, the nest floating in these freezing currents for weeks until it eventually found itself drifting into frozen waters off the coast of Iceland.

The ocean currents were faster now and as the weeks turned into months and as the icebergs it had now befriended drifted with it to the south, the nest turned to remaking and reshaping itself. It found it needed some sort of ballast, it wanted some underwater extrusions to help it stabilise itself. So as the nest drifted down towards the North Atlantic Ocean, it began to try out several new forms. One set of shapes that it tried over and over to realise were extensions of the human creatures that it remembered had been part of its earlier lives. It tried and tried but never really got the shapes quite right, arms would bend in the wrong place and legs just seemed too awkward. It eventually settled for a simple fin that it copied from the creatures that swam past.

All this remodeling took time and while the nest was finding out how to build and reform and reconnect all the various elements in its body, it had floated down through Canadian waters and was now to be found floating off the east coast of the United States of America, just off the island tip of New York city and the nest began to notice another change. It had not seen so much plastic in the water for a long time, not since it had passed through a city on a river many months before.

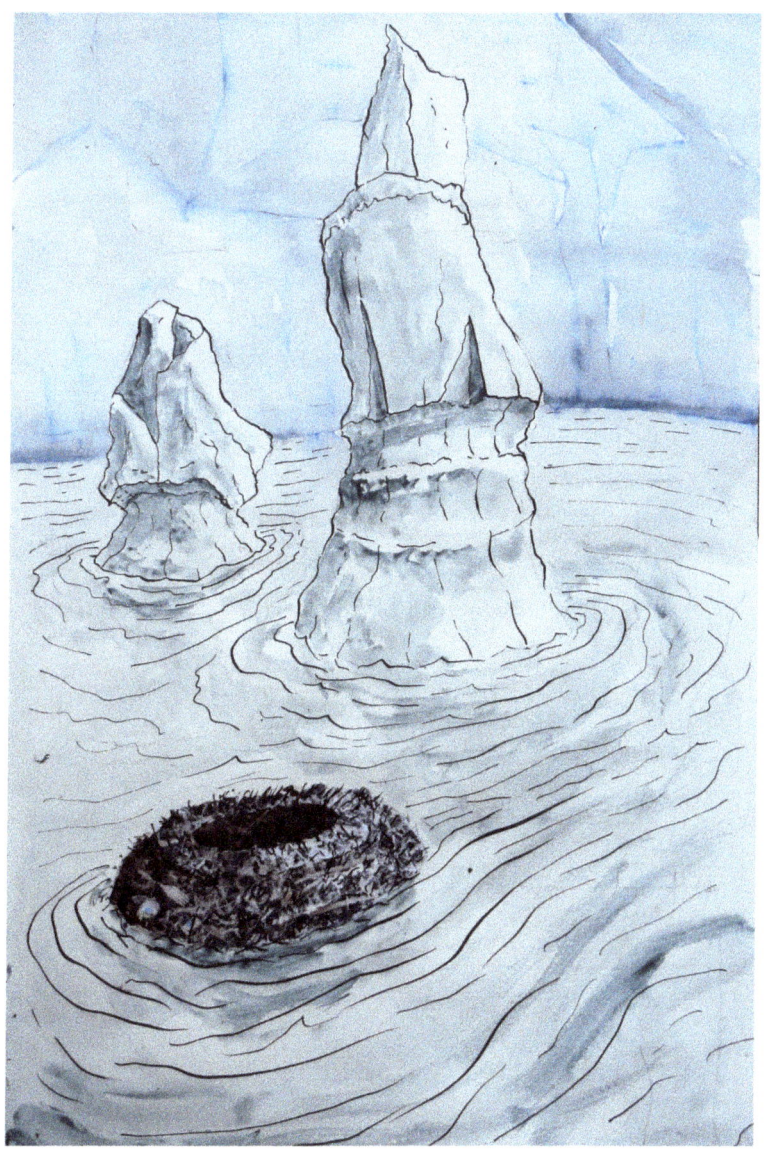

There were almost too many bottles, too much thread and broken plastic for it to cope with, all it could do was to hold out its feelers and net anything that would let itself be netted. As it did it picked up more and more material lives and wove them all into its own. The bigger it became the more it had to think about, every new component brought its own story which the nest added into the material memories of the whole. Its material intelligence was expanding, it became more and more aware of more and more types of materials and each material had a different story, one that the nest realised it could remember by simply passing through each component a very weak electrical charge.

But soon the nest was swept back into the deep ocean, it moved away from the coast as the Gulf Stream sent it back over the Atlantic, floating eastwards for several weeks, but then becoming becalmed for day after day, a time it passed by speaking to flying fish and tuna, to turtles and sharks and even to an albatross, each one of which it asked about the special island in the seas that it now sought out as its purpose. Only the albatross had news for it, a tale of a huge continent, one bigger than any other, lying in the middle of the ocean. The albatross also said that from what it had seen when it had flown over this continent, in many ways it was made of materials just like the nest.

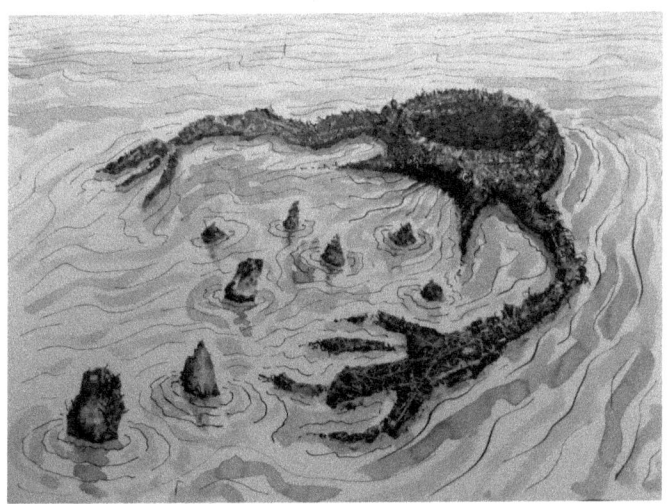

Soon the winds picked up, and the currents began to flow more quickly again. After a few more days the nest found itself floating in the waters that splashed onto the sandy beaches of Portugal and Spain, where as it floated south again, it collected empty bottles of suntan cream, broken polystyrene cups, cotton buds on plastic sticks and nylon fishing nets.

The weather was constantly changing, storms would alternate with hot sun and a balmy sea. One day a violent wind whipped up the ocean and the skies above into a raging ferment.

The sea churned, the nest plunged deep down into swirling hollows and then rose again atop mountainous waves, cresting into open space and was hurled out and down into the next submerging swell. Nothing it seemed could survive in this encounter with the elements. Again and again it was tossed up into the air and just as the nest was starting to think that was it, just as it was beginning to fall back down into yet another deep hollow, a wet bedraggled thump arrived right in its centre. A thing from the skies that had once been able to fly but was now so wet and storm confused that it had aimed for the only spot in a wide sea that looked vaguely like a bird's nest, something that shouldn't be there, something that must be a last moment vision, the one place it might survive. Nest drew itself in and covered its new addition, and rode out the storm as a tightly furled ball.

Eventually the storm passed, the nest returned to its usual form and a sodden, oil streaked gull pulled its head out from under its wing and looked out at the world. It soon tried to fly but in its last dip into the waters before it landed it had hit an oil slick and its wings and body were matted and sticky with unnatural oils, oils that during its collapsed exhausted sleep, had worked their way up through its feathers and had coated it in brown.

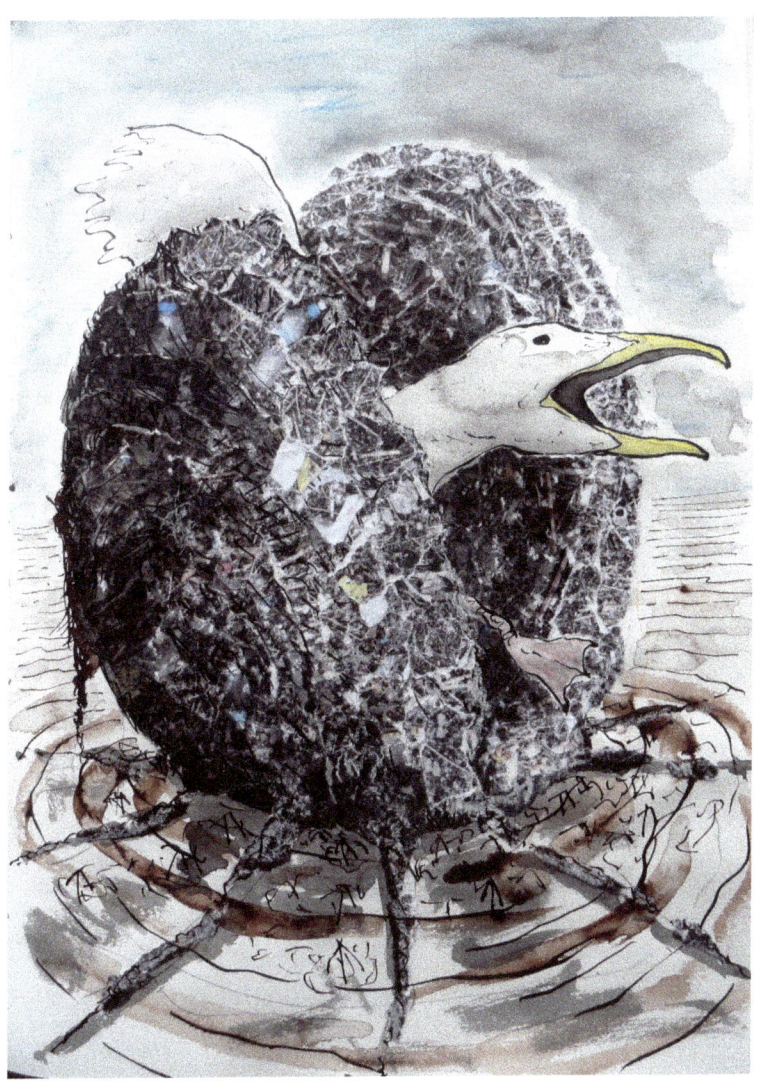

Nest sensed the gull's panic and fear, and in response began singing a swan song that its makers had sung all that time ago when they had their hatchlings to care for. Nest remembered how the song had calmed the tiny cygnets and had washed away their fears, and the throating sound of long necked swan vibrations was recreated, this time in the middle of a choppy sea, a sound made by the rubbing together of plastics and wire and the nest's own version of an aeolian harp, thin tendrils of cellophane, stretched across a broken bottle. Once the gull had calmed down, nest began to speak with it. "It's going to be all right, I understand your problem and I can solve it, but you will have to be brave". The gull had no choice in the matter being coated in oil and helpless; all it could do was nod in assent, believing it must still be in a dream or was already dead, arriving in an afterlife of monstrous ghostly nests. The nest now extended little feelers of plastic, working tiny filaments into amongst the bird's feathers, swabbing and sucking the surface oil away. But then it needed to get in deep, to put away the oils that had penetrated far down into the bird's skin and to do that it would need to cocoon the gull in a ball of tendrils and immerse it in a chemical cleaning body. To do this it needed to reshape itself, and by pushing and straining and straining and pushing suddenly with a noise of polystyrene snap, and wire grating it folded itself in two.

The scene looked like a gull in a giant fly trap. The startled bird tried to beat its wings, it tried to cry out but in that moment it had been totally immersed in wires that bound it tight, in feelers and filaments that would scour every speck of oil from its body, as a chemical fog drifted through every feather of its being. It was as if suddenly mummified. Then before the bird could pass out in either fright or suffocation, with another great snap Nest sprang back out into its former shape, as it did so catapulting the gull straight up into the cold fresh air, where now flapping madly the gull felt the air catch in its wings and it flew again. It spiralled up into the air, breathed deeply and looked back down at a now more recognisable nest and as it dived and dipped back towards what it had thought at first to be a dream, it squawked, "More warning would have been nice, but thank you for everything, especially my life." Nest replied that it was nothing and that it had used the oil it had cleaned from the bird's feathers to lubricate itself. The oil would help its movement through the water and would protect its metal parts. Before it flew away the gull offered to help the nest out at any time of future need; coughing up from its stomach a beautiful round shiny stone. "If you are ever in trouble," it squawked, "just toss this stone into the water and wherever you are, I will send help". Thank you replied the nest and it tucked the stone down with the others and waved its tendrils in goodbye as the gull flew off towards the far away Spanish shore.

The nest now floated past the entrance to the Mediterranean and as it did so it felt itself pushed westward again, back into deep waters, out into the Atlantic Ocean but then, after just four days of moving west, it became becalmed, slowly turning in circles as a soft breeze touched its upper reaches and it bobbed gently up and down. The gentle motion of an almost imperceptible ocean swell was rocking the nest to sleep. As it did so, it began to dream, as only a creature of its sort could, of the ancient land of Pangaea, of giant swamps and dog-sized dragon flies. Of a Carboniferous life that seemed to last for ever, it dreamt of changes in the planet's air and rocks and weather forms. It dreamt of strange forests of giant ferns, of rotting vegetation, of layers of earth and soil and fungi and of rocks and dust and fossils made and fossils lost, of years and years of seas that grew and shrank again, of animals that climbed up trees and disappearing mountains. But most of all it dreamed of black and oily substances that squeezed between the rocks, of carbon chains and coal and gas and polymerization. It dreamed the lives of polystyrene and acrylic and nylon and rayon and polyvinyl chloride, of polypropylene and polythene and Styrofoam, of polyethylene and polycarbonate, and all the other types of plastic forms included in the nest.

V

The nest dreamed on, but gradually what was a dream of connections and entanglements, became a nightmare of invisible monsters and unseen threats.
Something was happening, something had disturbed the nest and was shaking it out of its dreamy sleep, its sensors were quivering, and it wasn't sure whether it was still dreaming or whether it had woken. Whatever was happening it seemed to involve a big white shape looming up out of the ocean. It was becoming bigger and bigger and not just because it was getting nearer and nearer. It was there and then not there, between each appearance it would dive down below the waves and as it rose up out of the sea, before plunging back into the waves again, the nest caught glimpses of a huge mouth many yards across. A mouth that could open so wide that the nest realised it could swallow it's whole world down all in one gulp. What could it do? It couldn't swim away, it couldn't defend itself, or change its shape in time to hide or talk its way around and out of trouble. The creature now rose from the waters again and fell back down into the sea, as it surged on towards the nest. Waves from the plunge down of its huge white body were already violently rocking the nest as the thing emerged back out of the foaming sea and as it rose once more the nest saw its gaping jaws and its many teeth that glistened most fearfully in its cavernous mouth.

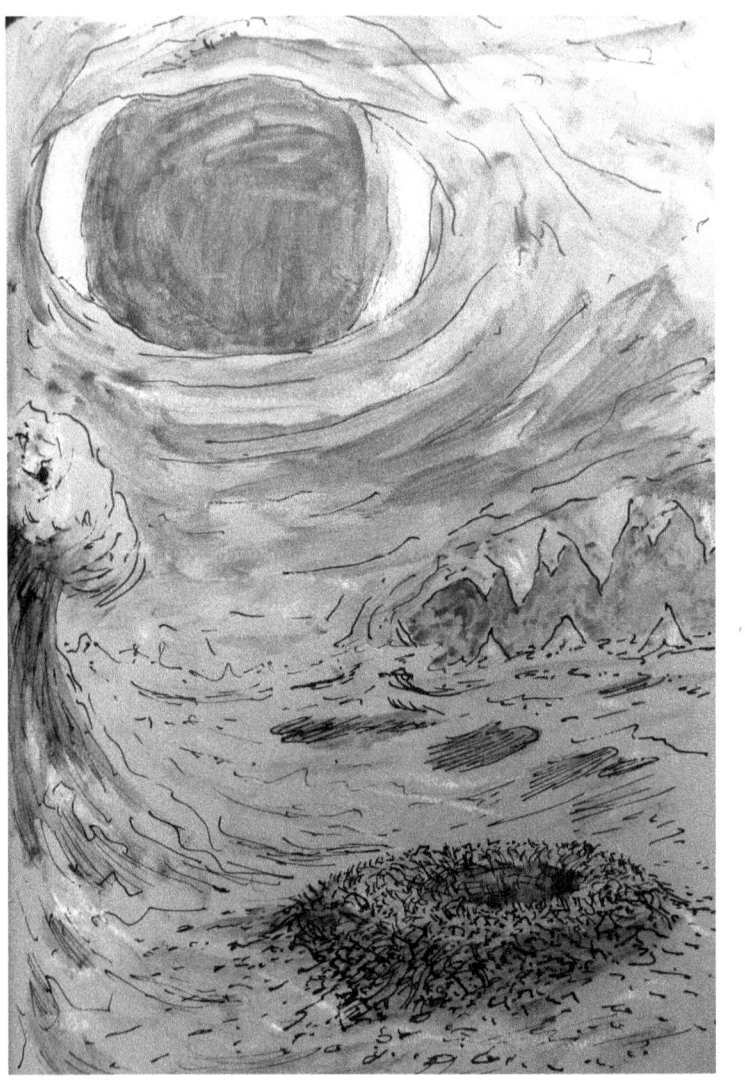

There was only one thing the nest could think to do, it reached deep down inside itself, and found the four pebble tokens that had been given it for good deeds done and kindness shown. Wrapping them in a broken net, it swung them around in as wide a circle as it could manage, and then it let go of the net, and the stones flew off towards the huge monster. But they fell well short and they dropped together making a very insignificant splash as they passed through the churning foam of the sea. The monster now grew ever nearer, its mouth getting ever wider, its churning form rocking the nest and disorientating its senses of space and time. Dizzy and hypnotised by the white mass and its glistening teeth, the nest was terrified. But then an eerie sound began, a whistle or a murmur, that hadn't been there just moments before. The ocean was bending and slipping down right in front of the huge creature, it dipped and twisted, and became a whirlpool, growing wider and wider and deeper and deeper. The monster then too late saw the problem, it began to try and change direction, but its mass was far too huge to make a sudden change of direction. Its mouth closed, its eyes once focused into tiny slits, now wide open and staring out in fear. Then as suddenly as it had appeared it was gone, sucked down into the depths, depths that seemed to go down forever, depths that somehow the nest remained on the edge of, whirling around and around a deepening hole as it spiralled out of sight.

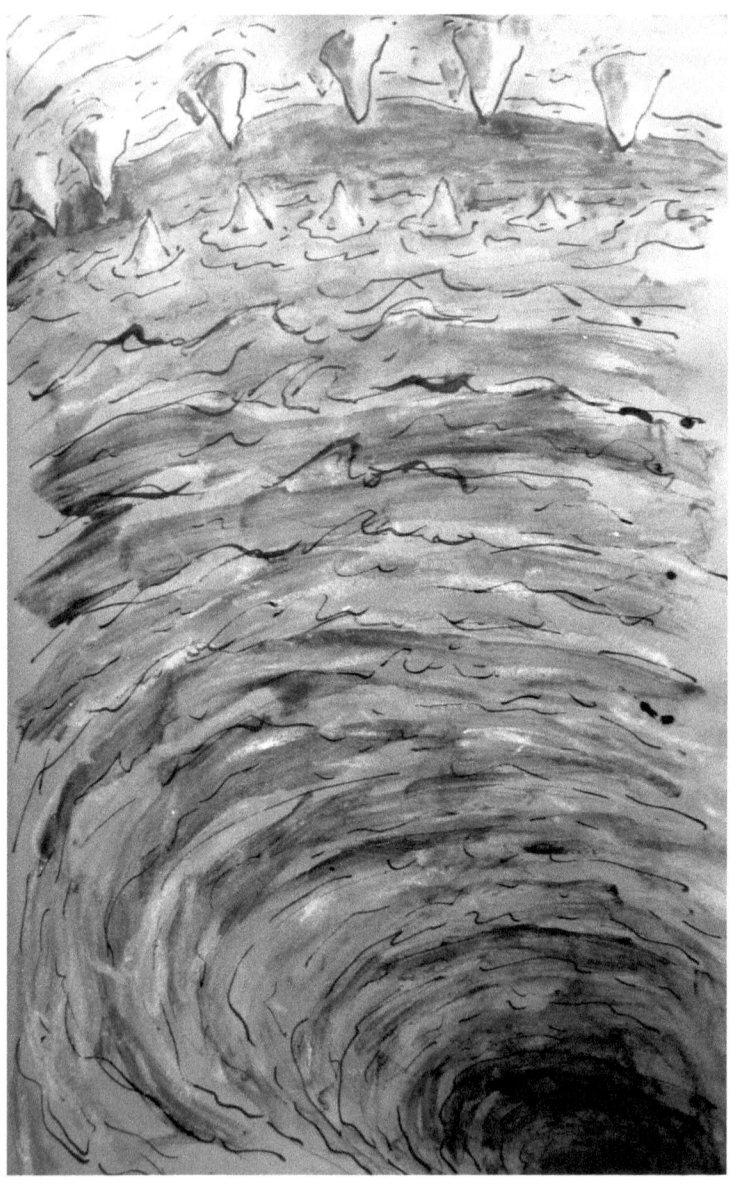

Now something was rising, rising from the whorl of water, coming up, from the depths. At first the nest thought it was the monster, coming back to finish the job of swallowing it, but as it rose its shape was changing and a great huge genii began to form itself out of the air and whirling waters. Then as the genii found its form it whirled around the edges of the nest, formed almost human hands and with them carried it aloft.

The genii rose, and carried the nest with it, until they were far above the ocean. For the first time the nest was flying and it realised how the swans must have felt as they flew and why they had to leave the earth. It looked down and saw what was below and the nest began to form an image of something in its mind of a possible future.

The genii now spoke to the nest, it said its name was Gaia, and that it lived as part of ocean and as part of earth, but mainly of the ocean, which is what the earth is really called. "Look down" it shouted and it pointed out the continent below. A slowly churning, spinning mass of plastics and every other type of flotsam and jetsam that had ever been thrown away by humans and abandoned to the seas, was floating and sinking and being pulled apart as fast as it clumped together. Gaia told the nest that humans by manipulating the carbon chains of life had begun a process that they were now no longer in control of, this north Atlantic gyre, this "garbage patch" was now bigger than the size of the land continents of India and Europe combined.

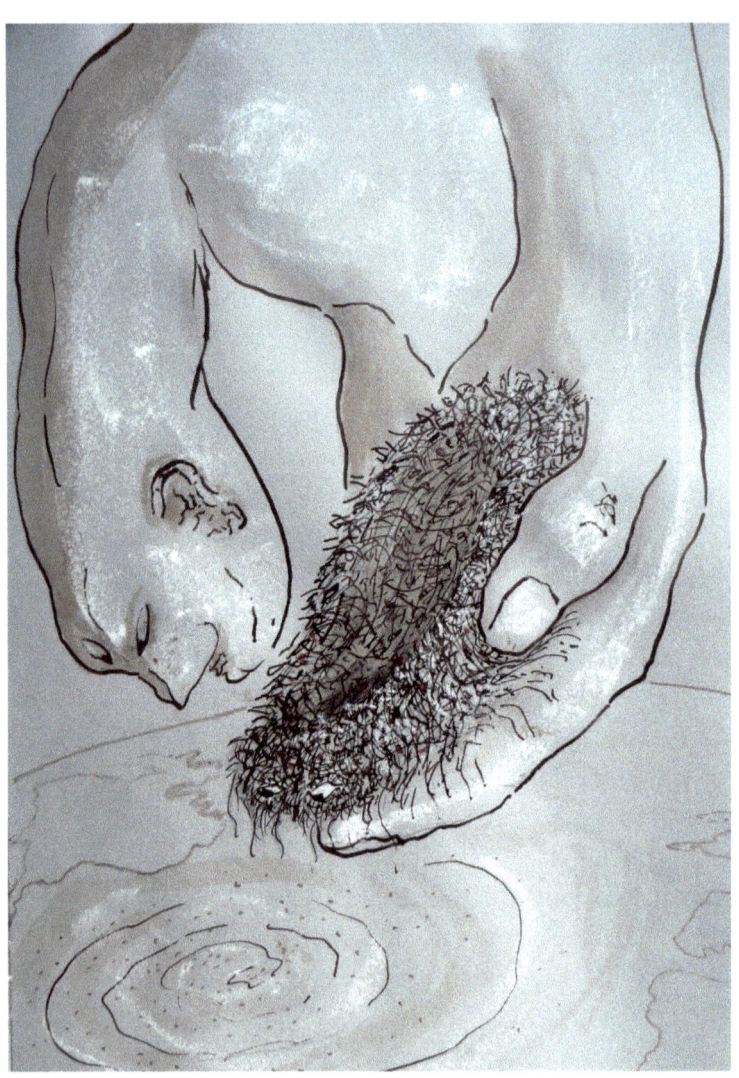

It was now so huge, so full of vibrant materials and had built itself into such a twisted complex of interconnections, that all it now needed was a spark to ignite it, to jolt it into life and that now the nest had arrived the necessary catalyst was here. This, Gaia said, was what the nest had been made for, that slowly turning mass of debris down there in the ocean was waiting for it, waiting for the nest to give it life and begin a new era in the life of plastic.

The genii was dropping down now, and the nest found itself heading towards the centre of a gigantic continent of plastic waste, a supersized gyre, a gyre where size matters, a collection of plastic matter of a size unheard of before. This, thought the nest, is the richest resource on Earth. A resource discarded by humans, but one the nest could work with.

As it entered the mass of plastic rubbish it made connections with it. Its nets and strings and feelers, touched and rubbed against plastics of many forms and shapes and compositions. Its connections and linkages, began to weld together something that would grow to be bigger than India, bigger than Europe, bigger than India and Europe combined. Colossal entanglements of circuitry, began to be woven into a labyrinthine knot of material combinations.

A continent sized saline battery was charged and made active, as electromagnetic bonds were pulled apart and rebuilt. Threads of plastics became nervous systems, systems so fine and yet so gigantic that all the rivers of the world could not compete with their combined length. The nature of this new physicality was emerging and as it did so it began to form an image. The nest had begun to imagine something, it saw a shape in its mind, one that began with a tiny electrical charge, a charge that was directed through a colossal maze of complex circuitry. Layers of electrons began to be realigned, atoms formed new connections and molecules were recharged. A gigantic plastic life form was emerging from the ocean and it was an idea, it had a form to go with that idea and an emerging materials mind to give shape to it.

Nearly all the memories that the nest had were to do with things that had been discarded and thrown away, they were memories about being no longer wanted. It now had a collection of billions of reminiscences about being treated as waste and rubbish and litter. But one of the earliest swan built parts of its construction had a different memory, one that was about love and care and a vision. One small green plastic nozzle had once been part of a boy's plastic toy rocket, one made from an empty washing up liquid bottle. The plastic nozzle remembered a time when a small boy had lavished great care on it. The boy had cleaned the bottle, soaked it in water to remove the stuck on paper label, carefully shaped some cardboard fins and had played with it for many months. The bottle had been to the moon and back, had reached the stars and even went beyond the galaxy. The boy had eventually lost his spaceship in a stream he had been playing in and this was why it found itself floating in the river, by accident rather than by design. This was one of the first ideas that had helped the nest find a model for what it wanted to do. It could now shape that idea and share with all its billions of parts an idea of leaving an earth that had so many bad memories for the entire entanglement.

Over the next few months, as connections were made, atoms exchanged and circuits grown something marvellous was happening. The nest made itself into a giant tube, several miles thick and inside that tube it became hotter and hotter, until a furnace was roaring, a furnace like the sun, a sun the nest now knew had given life to all on earth. Inside the furnace new materials were made and as they were they were moved back down into the fibrous structure of the nest, tiny sinews grew and strengthened and twisted around each other until fresh new forms were grown. Forms that included millions of feet of lost circuitry, once stamped into plastic circuit boards now reformed as part of an extended nervous system. Forms that flexed and thought, that controlled temperature, that breathed in chemicals and exchanged them for new ones, forms that could generate their own electro-chemical baths, tendrils of inorganic DNA entwined with organic matter and infused with metallic salts.

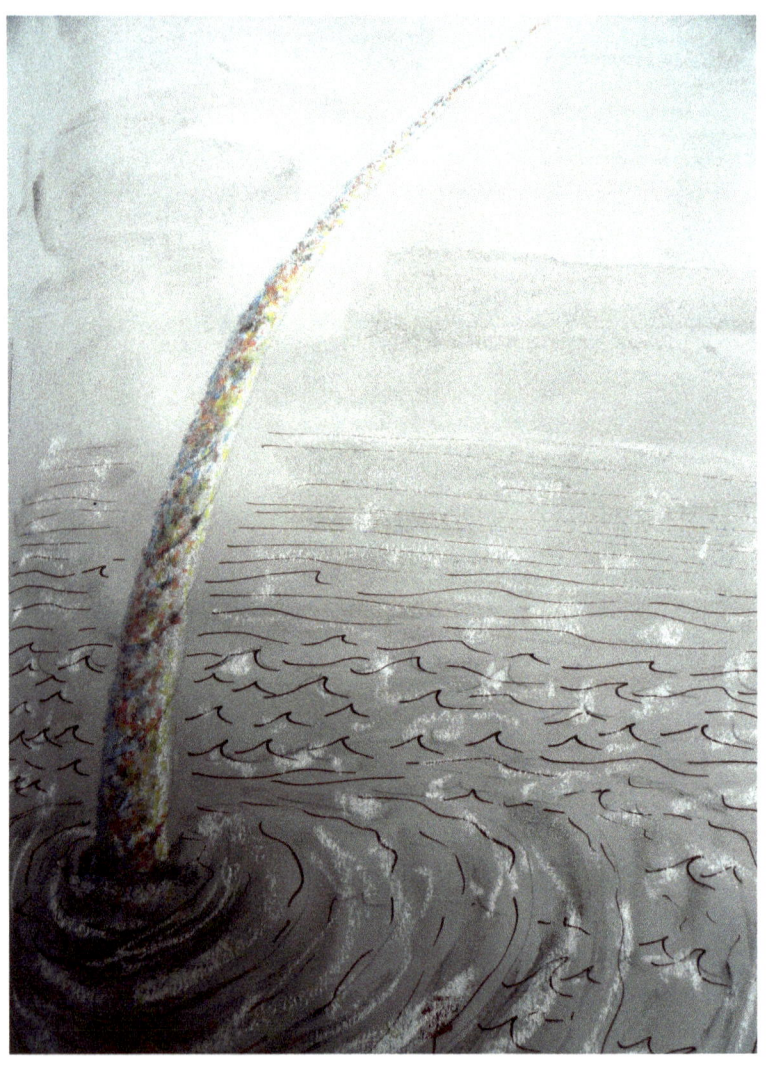

Like an earlier primordial soup, the gyre had made its own chemical bath, a bath of life potential that now was birthing something huge and with a purpose.

Slowly a curved dome began to emerge from the ocean. It rose up and gradually its sides became steeper, and as these sides emerged from the sea, they shimmered with rainbow light, its surface was multi-coloured, like an iridescent butterfly wing. As it raised itself higher and higher it looked more like a long glowing tube with a rounded end. It continued to rise and the sea churned around its base as it performed unimaginable physics and chemistry beneath the waves. Higher and higher it was reaching, until the tube from a distance began to look more like a thread or a thin line, a thread that when you got up close you realised was actually at least two miles thick. The line continued moving upwards, all day and all night it rose. Eventually it left the air of the Earth behind, it moved out into space and as it did it reached towards the moon. Like that boy who many years ago had in his imagination tried to sail his plastic spaceship into space, the nest was now stretching out to reach the nearest celestial object. It had learnt to fish and had entangled many a fishing line into its nervous system, so had fishing in its plastic veins and was now looking to catch hold of the circling moon.

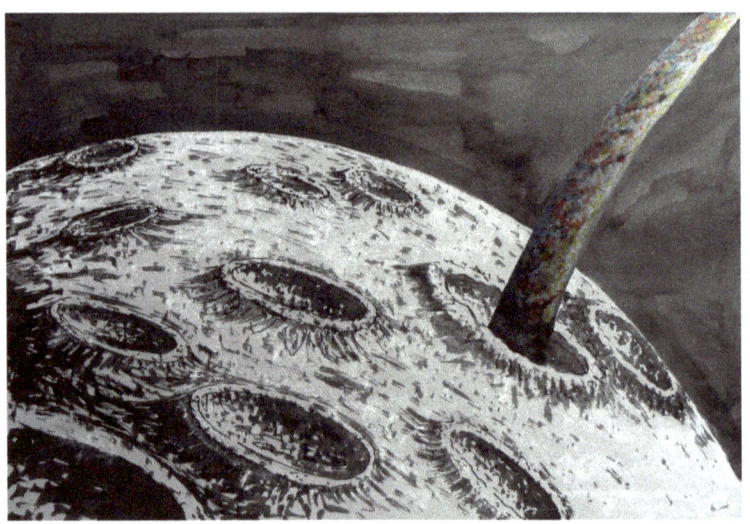

The tube of nest, the spaceship of plastic imagination threaded its way out into space, its dome shaped top slowly transforming into a giant hook. However it was now so long that it had to fight really hard to stop itself from breaking apart. But the moon was getting closer and closer. As the moon came round the earth, the thread could now touch its surface, and as it did so its giant hook felt for a hole in the edge of a moon crater and snagged itself into a mile wide crevice. As it did so it was jerked taut, it was stretched to its limit but before it could break its tail pulled itself clear of the ocean.

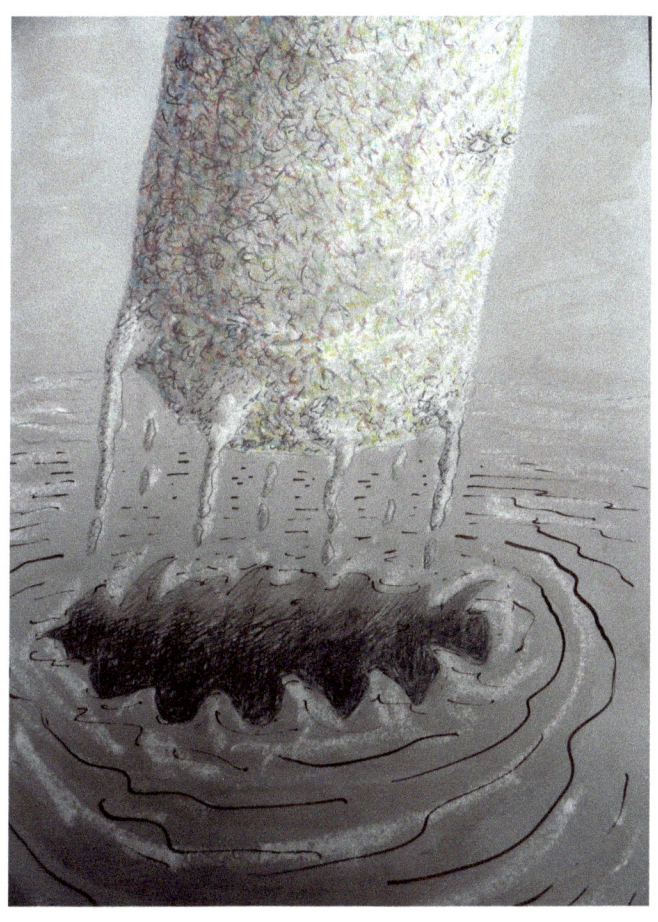

A two miles wide hollow, made as the water released it, was the last impact the nest would ever make upon the Earth.

The moon now reeled it in, the long line of the nest's tubular body now spiralling around itself as it laid itself down into the hollow crater that was to be its new home. As it rebuilt itself from its own spiralling form it made itself a nest again, a nest that remembered above all the swans and how they flew and their long thin necks as they circled round the nest as it first grew, and above all else their kindness in its making.

So now you know why it is, that if you look carefully at the moon on a cloudless night, you might, if you squint up your eyes really tightly, just manage to see a moon crater that could, with a little imagination, look like a huge nest. If you look even harder you might even be able to see a clutch of what would be gigantic eggs, waiting to hatch.

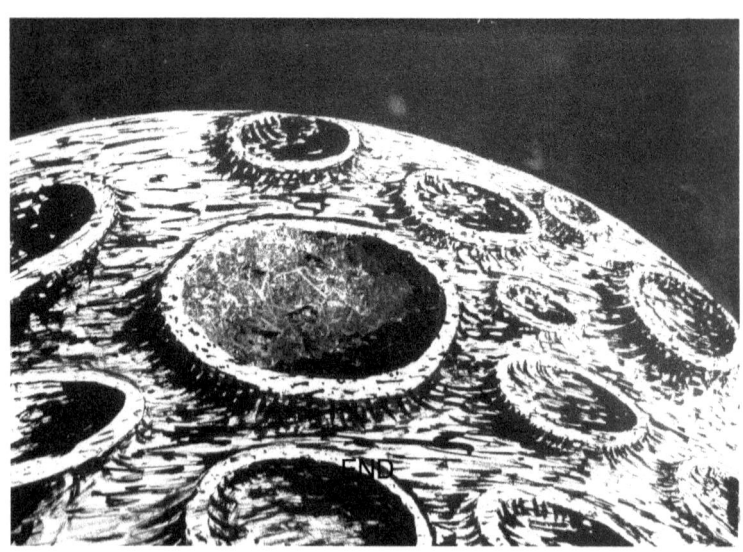

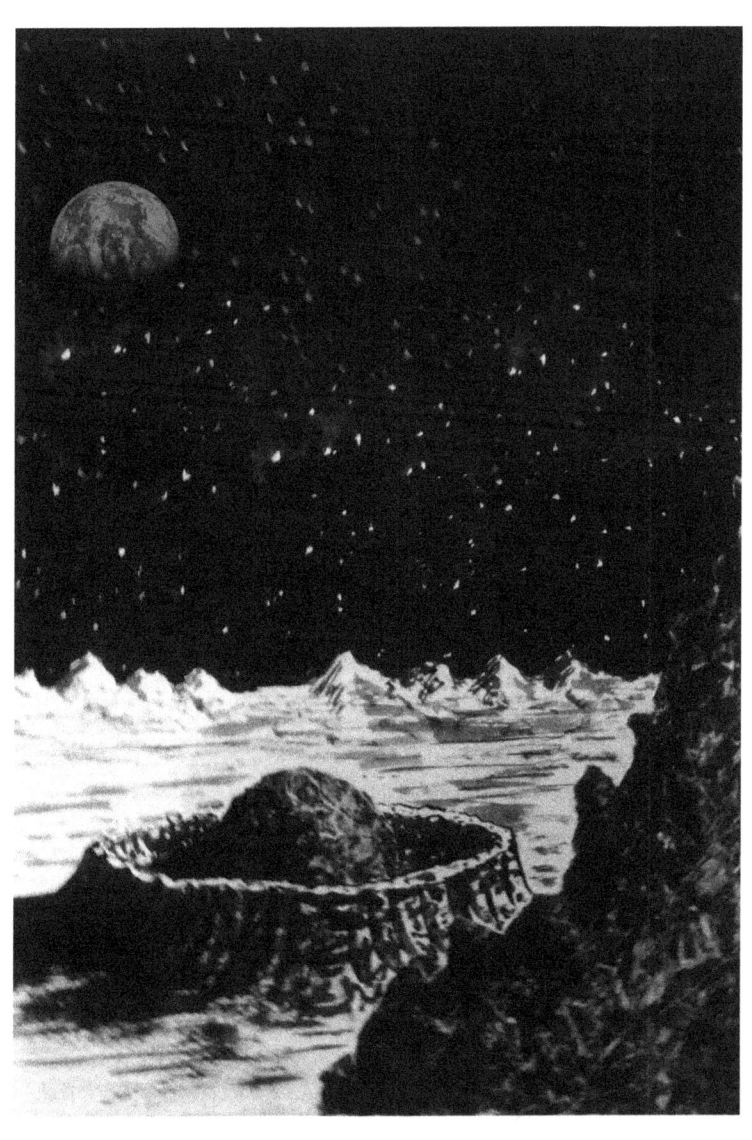

END

Afterword

This story emerged from work done for an exhibition in Wakefield, in the county of West Yorkshire in England, called (im)Material Disarray. The exhibition allowed me to extend my thinking about how I could as an artist respond to sustainability issues. The gallery was housed in a former domestic space and it seemed appropriate to make all my work by recycling things from around my own house and studio. As I had to visit the gallery several times, first of all to get an idea of the space and then to install work, I became familiar with the city and one place in particular began to intrigue me, a space where the road network crossed over a divide in the river Calder. This space was isolated by roads and the river had been divided to enable a weir to control water flow. This meant a slowing of the current and a building up of collections of rubbish that had been thrown into the river as it had passed through the city. One day when I looked down into this cut off area of watery wasteland I saw two swans at work building a nest, and because there was so much rubbish down there, they were making most of the nest out of it. This didn't seem to phase them, and the swan on the nest at the time, was carefully pulling into the space around itself all sorts of cartons, bits of plastic, string and anything else within its bill's reach.

Over the time of exhibition I visited the nest several times to make drawings and the swans went on to lay eggs and look after them. When I visited several weeks later everything had gone, there was no evidence of the nest.

As part of the exhibition I had promised to develop some sort of performative event and I decided to tell a story that had begun to be formulated in my head about the swans and their nest building, because their work seemed a much more resonant and appropriate response to sustainability than the work I had made out of rubbish myself.

I told the story one Sunday afternoon to a small gathering in the gallery and it seemed to be received very well by those there, the story you have just read, had its bare bones sketched out that day, but then on reflection decided to push it through to some sort of conclusion. Making drawings using collaged elements taken from photographs taken at the time of rubbish in the area, I decided to use these drawings to construct the story and organise them as a storyboard to work from.

But not being a writer, I was very happy that when I completed my first draft my nephew, Sam, who is a writer, then expressed an interest. He then kindly rewrote it and sent it back to me. It was much better but it was now in his more sophisticated voice, so I rewrote it again, baring in mind how he had added or changed some sections.

It was becoming a collaborative piece and this was fine because all my works are collaborative in that they arrive out of conversations, with people, materials and in this case two birds.

So thank you Paula Chambers for envisioning the exhibition, Jane Bryant of SNAPart for hosting it, the two swans for feeding my story and all of the materials I used to make the work, materials that came into my life to do certain things and ended up doing other things, but most of all thank you Sam for rewriting everything and then being faced with me rewriting it all again, never complained.

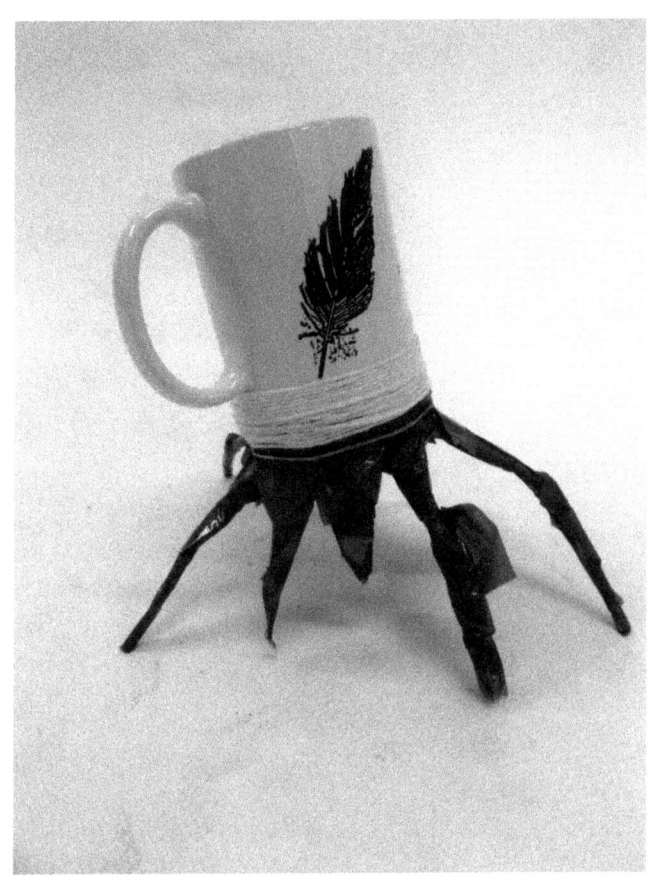

www.ingramcontent.com/pod-product-compliance
Lightning Source LLC
Chambersburg PA
CBHW040518220526
45473CB00012B/2907